Tony And His Mythical Friends

Tony was so excited. His mom signed him up for summer camp at Double Lake Mountain. He rode the bus with the same buddies that he enjoyed camp with last year.

"Hey, let's sing our old camp song again, hopefully you did not forget it," said Nate.

"I remember it very well. Let's sing it together!" said Tony and they sang happily. Everyone was cheerful and laughing including Camp counselor Dave who grew a lot taller since the last time Tony saw him. Tony's friend Bailey was also on the bus. She had a funny laugh, "Neighe-he-he!" It made them laugh louder every time they heard it. Andrea was there too. She was the best swimmer in the group. She could not wait to get in the water. Tony noticed Toby was not participating much in the sing-along. He recently got a new pair of special shoes that helped him walk better but it made him uncomfortable. Tony tapped Toby on the shoulder, smiled and began to sing the old camp song louder. It changed Toby's mood. Toby cheered up and joined the sing-along.

Everything at Double Lake Mountain looked the same as last year. Setting up camp was fun. Robbie always got himself tangled in his tent and it was so funny to see him roll on the floor trying to get out. The first night was filled with clear skies and lots of stars.

"Does anyone know any scary stories?" said Robbie.

"I don't like scary stories," said Nate.

"OK, Let's tell each other some funny jokes instead," said Tony.

They told each other the silliest, most ridiculous jokes. Every time Bailey laughed, "Neighe-he-he," it made the friends laugh louder until their bellies hurt. Everyone went into their tents for the night.

"Goodnight," said Robbie.

"Goodnight," said Tony.

"See you in the morning," said Nate.

"I can't wait for breakfast tomorrow. Goodnight!" said Andrea.

Tony could not fall asleep. He kept looking at the top of his tent, when suddenly he heard a noise.

He peeked out of his tent to see if there was an animal nearby but did not see one. So, he climbed out of his tent. Tony saw a shadow running into the woods. In fact, there was more than one. He could hear their whispers but could not understand what they were saying. Their voices sounded like children.

Tony then saw a flickering light. The light was very dim and far behind a row of trees in the woods.

"What is that?" he whispered to himself. He could no longer see the shadows. Tony continued to walk through the woods. As he got closer, Tony noticed there was another campsite.

"Did I just walk around in a circle back to our camp?" Tony thought to himself. Tony compared campsites. In his camp, all the tents were the same height and width. Tony noticed this new camp had tents with all different shapes and sizes.

Tony slowly walked towards the middle of the campsite. *Where did they all go?* He heard all of them a few minutes ago.

"Hello? Anyone here? I am from the camp, just beyond the trees. My name is Tony." There was a sudden whisper. It was too low for Tony to understand. "I can't hear you very well. Would you please speak up?" said Tony.

Then a girl's voice replied, "Please go back to your camp."

Tony said, "Why do you want me to go back to my camp?"

The voice said, "We do not want to scare you. You will probably scream. We just want to enjoy our camping trip."

At first Tony thought, *Scream? Why would I be scared of another kid like me?* Then he said, "If I promise not to scream, would you please show yourself? Will all of you show yourselves?"

They all whispered, "YES."

Tony then said, "OK. I promise."

The voices in the tent started to whisper.

"You, go first..."

"No, you go first."

"I think it's better if she goes first."

"Let me go first."

"No, I should go first..."

Until one whisper declared, "I will go first."

Then rest all whispered at once... "Perfect!"

Tony was filled with anticipation. He knew he would not be scared. He saw their shadows and their whispers sounded just like children. Maybe this will turn out to be no big deal and both camps could get together to play fun games. Tony loved to meet new people and he was friends with everyone.

Tony could hear a zipper slowly unzip. Slowly one foot came out of a tent that was not so oddly shaped.

Tony squinted his eyes to get a better look. He could only see a girl with her back to him. She was about his height with two ponytails on each side of her head.

"Hi, my name is Cylee."

Then Tony said, "Hi, Cylee! My name is Tony. Why don't you turn around?"

Then Cylee said, "I'm afraid you will scream."

What could possibly be so different about Cylee? Tony thought. "I promised I would not scream or run away. Trust me."

"OK, here goes..." And slowly Cylee turned around. Finally, Tony saw her face. She had one big eye. It was shut. Tony could not believe it. A Cyclops? A real Cyclops? No way!

Tony smiled with excitement and said, "You're a Cyclops! I thought a Cyclops was just a mythical creature. This is so cool!"

Cylee's fear changed to excitement once she heard Tony's reaction. They just stared at each other. The others were still waiting in their tents. Cylee had never seen a real human up close before. "You didn't scream or run away. Thank you," said Cylee.

"Sure thing!" said Tony. "So can your other friends come out now?" Tony was excited to meet the others.

"Sure. Hey guys, come out. It's ok!" Cylee shouted. Tony's mind was racing. Who else is in those tents? Could it be an entire Cyclops Family? One by one the tents began to unzip. Suddenly, Tony became distracted by a loud splash in the pond.

At that moment he saw a girl's head come out of the water. She was not a regular girl. She had a fin. It was a Mermaid! Tony could not believe it!

Tony turned back towards Cylee and standing there were the rest of Cylee's friends. A Leprechaun, an Alicorn, a Bigfoot and a Faun. Tony's eyes and mouth were wide open with amazement.

They all said "Hi" at the same time.

Suddenly Tony started to breathe fast. "I need to sit down," he said. They helped him have a seat next to the campfire.

"Are you OK Tony? Do you want some water?" said Cylee.

"Good Idea" said the Bigfoot as he turned to the Leprechaun and said "Hurry, run over and get Tony some water from the lake."

"He can't drink that water!" The Alicorn said to the Leprechaun. "He's a human, he needs water from the stream."

"Ah yes, I will be right back." said the Leprechaun as he disappeared into another part of the woods. "Please don't faint Tony. You will be fine. We will take care of you," said the Faun.

Tony started to catch his breath. He looked up to get another look at the creatures he just met. Tony noticed the creatures were young just like his friends back at camp. "You guys are Mythical!" said Tony. "Mythical creatures don't really exist. They are just made up characters in a story. How is it that you are all here? How can you be real?"

"He's still in shock," muttered the Faun.

"We are Mythical Friends. We do not like to be called creatures because it makes us sound scary. We are not scary at all," said Cylee.

"We are not seen by humans at all, but for some reason you can see us." said Cylee. Just then the Leprechaun came over with a small bucket of water and gave Tony a full cup to drink from.

"Here you go Tony." Tony took the cup from him slowly all while studying his small body.

"Are you a Leprechaun?" asked Tony.

"Yes," replied the Leprechaun.

Then Tony pointed and said, "You're an Alicorn!"

"Neighhh. Yes, I am. My name is Alley" said the Alicorn.

"And you're a Faun, right?" said Tony

"That is correct. The name is Fred." said the Faun.

"Nice to meet you Tony, my name is Barry and yes, I'm a Bigfoot."

"And don't forget me over here!" said Mermaid waving her arm. "I'm Megan," she said, while splashing around with excitement.

"Wow!" said Tony. "I can't wait to tell the others what a cool camp this is. They would probably love to come over for a game night."

"Oh no Tony! You can't tell anyone we are here," said Cylee. "We are not supposed to be seen by humans. We thought we would be invisible to you but for some reason we're not."

"Maybe he has special powers," said Megan. "Do you, Tony?" Cylee said to Tony as he started to stand up.

"Do I what?" said Tony.

"Do you have special powers?" said Cylee.

"If you mean superhero powers? I wish I could shoot lasers from my eyes or webs from my wrists. That would be so awesome! But no, I do not have any powers," said Tony

"We were about to enjoy a delicious snack, does this mean we can't now that Tony is here?" said Louie.

"I can show you how it's done, I love s'mores!" said Tony excitedly. Tony helped the Mythical Friends put the marshmallows on the sticks he found for roasting over the campfire. Tony also found a long stick that reached all the way out to Megan in the pond. She was so amazed at Tony's kindness. He found a way to include her and that made Megan feel special. Tony and his Mythical Friends enjoyed roasting the marshmellows as they told each other silly stories. They laughed so much. It was such a fun time.

Tony started feeling very tired and he suddenly fell into a deep sleep.

"What do we do now Cylee?" said Fred. "He cannot stay here. His camp friends will come looking for him soon and we don't know if they have the ability to see us like Tony does."

"We have to get him back to his camp," said Alley.

"Perhaps I can fly him on my back, and I'll lean to my side, so he'll fall down right on his tent," said Alley.

"You can't do that. He'll get hurt!" said Barry.

"No that won't work. We need to get to their campsite and put Tony in his tent without waking him or his camp buddies. But how will we do that?" said Megan. They all sat quietly wondering how this could be done.

"Let's keep it simple. We will lay him on top of Alley and together we will walk slowly to his camp. Megan, you can swim over and keep a watchful eye and let us know if anyone wakes up so that we can quickly hide in the woods," said Cylee.

"Absolutely, I will make a huge splash to let you know when you need to hide," said Megan.

"We need to go right now," said Fred. Using the blanket Tony was laying on, the Mythical Friends lifted him on to Alley's back face down. They all walked slowly through the woods, making sure Tony did not fall off. They reached the campsite to find all of Tony's camp buddies still sound asleep in their tents.

Barry lifted Tony off Alley and carried him to his tent with Cylee, Fred and Louie right behind him. Alley stayed back near the woods. Step by step the Mythical Friends walked. They were careful not to step on any branches or dry leaves that might wake the campers. They finally reached Tony's tent which was the only one open. They all helped Barry put Tony in his tent.

Suddenly, one of the campers shouted, "Hey, hey, hey cut it out! It's my turn now!" The Mythical Friends stood frozen. Their hearts were racing. Barry slowly turned his head from left to right to see who was speaking and he could not see anyone. He then quickly looked at Megan who raised her hand out of the water and shrugged her shoulders, letting them know there were no campers awake. Barry saw the worried look on Cylee, Louie and Fred's face and whispered, "I don't see anyone. The talking has stopped. Hurry, we have to go."

Quickly, they all stepped out of the tent. They walked back on the same path. Barry, Fred, Louie and Cylee reached the woods where Alley stood waiting for them. Their work was done. Megan swam back to their side of the pond. All the Mythical Friends walked silently back through the woods.

Tony woke up to the sounds of laughter and talking outside of his tent. There was a delicious smell of breakfast in the air. Tony sat up and stretched his arms wide. He started to remember last night and the fun he had with his Mythical Friends. *How did they bring me back to my tent?* he thought.

He jumped up and ran out of his tent. He rushed right passed Nate. "Hey, Tony, it's time for breakfast!"

But Tony just ran by. He also passed Robbie just as he went into the woods. Robbie was holding a bunch of twigs he had collected for the campfire.

"Are you ok Tony?" said Robbie.

"Yes, yes, I'm ok. I'll be right back," said Tony.

Robbie shook his head while laughing he said, "Someone has to go bad! Good luck buddy!"

Tony ran towards the tree lined path that lead to the Mythical Friends' campsite.

Tony was hoping so much to see the tents from last night, in the same position with their different shapes and sizes. But there was nothing. He ran to the spot where the campfire was set up by the Mythical Friends. There was nothing. Tony then looked out to the pond. Megan was gone.

Was it a dream? Tony thought to himself. He remembered Cylee saying the first hello, Louie bringing him water, Megan splashing around, Alley and Barry too. Tony suddenly felt sad because he did not get a chance to say goodbye. Tony wanted his Mythical Friends to know he would always be their friend.

Tony walked back. He saw Robbie still picking up sticks. In that moment, Tony noticed something. Robbie looked like *Cylee! How could that be?* Tony thought. Robbie had on goggles in the shape of one large oval that covered both his eyes. They made him look like a Cyclops! Tony never noticed it until now. The shirt, the hair color, the goggles. It was just like Cylee. Tony then walked to the campfire where everyone was sitting around finishing their breakfast.

"Tony, I saved you some breakfast," said Nate. Tony blinked his eyes and rubbed them. He could not believe what he was seeing. As Nate came towards him with a plate of food Tony was reminded of Louie! Nate was not as short as Louie, but he was the shortest of all the camp buddies. Nate was wearing the same colored clothes and a hat just like the one Louie wore. Tony could not stop staring at his hat.

Tony sat down to eat his breakfast. He kept looking at all his buddies. Unbelievable! He could see his Mythical Friends! Not only did Robbie look like Cylee and Nate looked like Louie. But Toby looked like Fred, Andrea looked like Megan and Camp counselor Dave looked just like Barry. They were almost the same height! Then there was sweet Bailey and her very funny laugh. Tony knew exactly who she sounded like…Alley! Tony had the biggest smile on his face for the rest of the camping trip. His old friends became new again. Tony will never forget his Mythical Friends.

Dedication

Thank you to my husband, Anthony. You love me and support my every endeavor. I am blessed to walk this life with you by my side. To my daughter Isabella it was our conversation in the car that inspired this story. You also created the first drawings of all the Mythical Friends. Your artistry is a gift. To my daughters Kayla and Liliana, thank you for helping me. You were both so creative with naming characters and giving your perspective during this process. This book is my gift to you, my beautiful family. I love you all, more and forever.

Also, a special thank you to Stephanie Richoll. You are gifted. Your professionalism and commitment to this project was more than we could have imagined. We, the Valentin family, are forever grateful.

Made in the USA
Middletown, DE
19 July 2020